# The Four Seasons of Patrick

Susan Hughes

Red Deer Press

Published in Canada by Red Deer Press
195 Allstate Parkway, Markham
ON, L3R 4T8
www.reddeerpress.com

Published in the U.S. by Red Deer Press
311 Washington Street, Brighton,
Massachusetts 02135

Edited for the Press by Peter Carver
Cover image courtesy of Photos.com
Cover and text design by Daniel Choi

We acknowledge with thanks the Canada Council for the Arts, and the Ontario Arts Council for their support of our publishing program. We acknowledge the financial support of the Government of Canada through the Canada Book Fund (CBF) for our publishing activities.

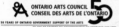 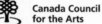

ONTARIO ARTS COUNCIL
CONSEIL DES ARTS DE L'ONTARIO
50 YEARS OF ONTARIO GOVERNMENT SUPPORT OF THE ARTS
50 ANS DE SOUTIEN DU GOUVERNEMENT DE L'ONTARIO AUX ARTS

Canada Council
for the Arts

Conseil des Arts
du Canada

Library and Archives Canada Cataloguing in Publication
Hughes, Susan, 1960-, author
    Four seasons of Patrick / Susan Hughes.
ISBN 978-0-88995-505-9 (pbk.)
    I. Title.
PS8565.U42F68 2013        jC813'.54        C2013-904214-8

Publisher Cataloging-in-Publication Data (U.S.)
Hughes, Susan.
    Four seasons of Patrick / Susan Hughes.
[80] p. : cm.
Summary When Patrick's father announces he is going to marry again and bring his new wife's seven-year-old daughter Claire into the family, Patrick is distressed. He and his friend Harry build a tree house where they can hangout without being bothered by Claire. It takes a while for Patrick to realize that Claire is also feeling out of her element, and he can help boost her spirits by offering her space in the tree house as well.
ISBN-13: 978-0-88995-505-9 (pbk.)
1. Children of divorced parents – Family relationships – Juvenile fiction. 2. Divorce – Juvenile fiction. 3. Stepfamilies – Juvenile fiction. I. Title
[Fic] dc23        PZ7.H84547 2013

Printed and bound in Canada by Friesens

MIX
Paper from
responsible sources
FSC
www.fsc.org        FSC® C016245

For my parents, Iris and Ray Hughes,

with all my love

# WINTER

# 1

## Snow Day

It was early Saturday morning. My eyes had just opened. Out my window, I saw the white tree tops. "Yippee!" I cheered. The first snow of winter was here—and on a Saturday, too!

I dressed quickly and raced downstairs. I was off to Harry's house. He's my best friend and we love the snow. That's why we have a winter tradition. On the first snowy day of the year, we play outside together all day long. We have our first snow fight, we make our first snowman, and we make our first toboggan run.

But Dad stopped me at the door. He had a plate of blueberry pancakes in one hand and a pitcher of maple syrup in the other.

"What about Harry and our tradition?" I asked.

"The snow tradition comes *after* the breakfast tradition," Dad told me with a grin.

I ate quickly, then bundled up. "See you later, Dad."

"Sure thing, Patrick," he said.

I was heading for the door when he added, "Oh, don't forget, Patrick. Linda and Claire are coming for dinner tonight."

"Again?" I complained. Linda and her seven-year-old daughter Claire had just been here for dinner two weeks ago. My chest felt tight. "I like it best when it's just the three of us—you and Trevor and me." Trevor's my older brother.

"I like that, too," Dad said, "but sometimes it's nice to have other people join us. Like your friend Harry, right? Sometimes you like to invite him for dinner." He paused. "Well, it's kind of the same for me with Linda."

I looked at Dad. It didn't seem at all the same to me. Harry had been my friend forever. Since before Mom died. When Harry came for dinner, he wasn't taking someone else's place.

But there was no way I wanted to talk about it. I didn't even want to think about it. And I could tell that Dad didn't really want to talk about it, either. Otherwise, he'd just do it. Talk, that is. Straight out. Like he usually did, no matter what it was, no matter whether I wanted to listen or not.

Plus, there wasn't time to talk. Not right now. Harry was waiting, and this was the first snowy day of the year. I wasn't going to let anything ruin that.

So I just shrugged and said goodbye to Dad. And he said goodbye again, too.

And then, finally, there I was, outside! I pulled the toboggan out of the shed. I started across the field of white. Harry lived on the next farm to ours, but it was a bit of a walk, especially through the snow.

Soon I saw him, a tiny dark speck in all that white. When I got closer, I could see more of him. He was sitting where he usually waited for me, on top of a fence rail. He saw me, too. Harry began to wave both arms. He jumped off the fence and ran. He was a comet, hurtling toward me, a tail of snow behind him.

When we were close, Harry yelled, "Take that!" He

threw a mittful of powdery snow at me.

I let go of the toboggan cord. I yelled, "Take *that*!" scooping snow in both hands and throwing it at him.

The fight was on. Snow flew through the air, a whirlwind, a snowstorm. Handfuls of it. Armfuls of it. It was in the air, flying in all directions. It felt like freedom. It was our first winter snow fight.

When we stopped, panting, we were covered from head to toe in snow.

"Ha! We're snowmen!" I told Harry. "Abominable snowmen!"

Harry and I stalked back and forth like abominable snowmen, our arms stiffly at our sides, our faces menacing. We gnashed our teeth and chanted, "We are Abominables! We are Abominables!"

Then, suddenly, we shook off the snow. "Time for our first toboggan run!" yelled Harry. "Let's go!"

We hurried across the frozen fields toward the pit.

But when we were almost there, we saw the snow tracks. They always have a story to tell.

I went first. "There are two sets," I said. "A fox and a

rabbit. So a fox and a rabbit come from two directions and they meet here." I pointed at a trampled area.

Harry pointed into the distance. "Only one set of tracks continues on. The fox caught the rabbit."

"And off he went," I said, ending the story.

We wanted to make our mark, too. So we stomped our names in the middle of a field.

PATRICK

HARRY

"An outer-space alien could read these letters," said Harry.

"Glad to meet you," I yelled up into space. "And what's *your* name?!"

We reached the steep snowy bank. The pit lay below, deep with snow. We were on top of the world.

"Yahoo!" I cried.

"Yahoo!" cried Harry.

We threw ourselves on the toboggan and shoved off. We swept down the hill. Whoosh! We flew like the wind!

Over and over again, Harry and I trudged up the bank and then hurtled back down the hill.

When our snow day was over, we said goodbye at

Harry's laneway.

"It was a perfect snow day," I said.

"Perfect," Harry agreed.

"Tomorrow's Sunday," I said.

"Yippee! We can do it all over again," said Harry.

I laughed. It's great having a friend who thinks the way you do.

## 2

### Star Memories

*I* didn't see Linda's car in the driveway. But maybe Dad had picked up Linda and Claire in our truck. Or maybe they were just late.

"They aren't coming tonight, after all," Dad said. "Claire's stomach is bothering her. They're going to come tomorrow night instead."

Dad's smile was more like a shrug. He was trying to make like he wasn't disappointed, but I could tell he was. This not showing up happened a lot. Claire seemed to get sudden colds or sore throats or fevers on the days that she and her mom were supposed to come here for dinner.

Anyway, I felt sorry for Dad, but it was fine by me. It

meant that at dinner, it was just Dad, Trevor, and me, after all. There was lots of room around the table. There was lots of space to talk. I got to tell Dad and Trevor about my snow day with Harry. About all our firsts.

"Sounds great," Dad smiled.

After we put away our dishes in the kitchen, I looked out the window. Darkness had settled on the farm.

Dad looked, too. "The sky is clear. Looks like a perfect star evening," he said. "Let's go for our walk, the three of us."

The snow-day tradition belonged to Harry and me. But my family has a tradition, too. The walk under the stars. We do it when the night is clear. We do it when the stars call out to us.

So we all bundled up. Together, Dad, Trevor, and I walked up the lane.

The tree branches stretched like bony skeletons above our heads. A farm dog barked way off in the distance.

Trevor wrapped the scarf around his face. Only his eyes peeked out the top.

I shivered. The insides of my boots were still wet from sledding.

Trevor talked about his first set of high school exams, which were coming up soon. Dad told a funny story about high school. He told about meeting Mom for the first time. He pretended to do her voice, teasing him. We all laughed.

We reached the road, where our world joined the wide world. Then we turned and walked back down our lane. We stood in the open yard outside our farmhouse, looking up at the sky, looking for the star.

Each season, the star moved. As time went on, it circled round and round overhead. It was hard for me to keep track of it. I always wanted to be the first one to spot it, but I never was.

Tonight, like always, Trevor saw the star before me. "There it is. Mom's star." He pointed.

Tonight, like always, Trevor told the story.

"It was a spring night and the sky was clear, like tonight. It was April. We didn't know yet that Mom was sick.

"We were all there, the three of us and Mom," Trevor went on. "We were all looking up at the night sky, looking at the stars."

Trevor told about Mom choosing the star. "She said: 'That star. That's the one.'"

My heart ached. I liked hearing the story, but I couldn't remember that spring night. I couldn't remember Mom before she got sick. I always felt left out, like I wasn't part of the story. Like there was room enough in that whole huge sky for Mom and Trevor and Dad, but not for me.

Trevor ended the story the way he always did. "And this is what Mom said to us:

'*Wherever I go, wherever I end up in this wide universe …*

*Wherever you go, wherever you end up in this wide universe …*

*That star will be our star.*

*That's the one that will connect us.'*"

The night air was quiet. Far away, the farm dog barked again.

"Okay, boys, time to go in now," Dad said. We climbed up the porch steps together.

I got ready for bed and, when I went to my room, I looked out the window at Mom's star. It connected us, sure. But I missed her, and I wished I could remember that night, and Mom not being sick.

# 3

## My Own Words

*T*he next day was Sunday. I looked outside. Yup, the snow still covered the fields and lay on the tree branches. Winter was here to stay.

Again, Harry and I played together all day. We went sledding at the snowy sand pit. We had lunch at Harry's house. Then, afterward, we played in the woods.

When we got to my house, Dad said I could invite Harry for dinner. He reminded me that Linda and Claire would be there, too.

"Who are they?" Harry asked as we washed up.

"Linda is just a friend of my dad's, I guess." I shrugged. "She lives in town. And Claire is her daughter. She's only seven. She's a pest."

Dinner was peas and mashed potatoes and chicken.

Claire threw peas at me when her mother wasn't looking. She kicked me under the table. She put gravy and potatoes in her mouth, chewed, and then opened her mouth so I could see in.

Harry grinned at her, but he was just being nice. She was so annoying.

"Thanks for the meal, Mr. McAllister," Harry told my dad. "My mom's going to pick me up soon. I better get ready." He said goodbye to Trevor. He said goodnight to Claire and Linda, too.

Linda pushed her chair back. She went round to Harry and held out her hand, all formal. "It was nice to meet you, Harry. It's good to meet a friend of Patrick's." Her voice was soft but steady, like she meant it.

Suddenly, it was too crowded inside. Harry went to put his winter jacket and his snow pants back on, and I put mine on, too. "I'll wait outside with you," I told Harry.

"Can I come, too?" Claire asked, suddenly beside me, pulling on my sleeve.

"No," I said.

"Please?" she asked. Her eyes were bright blue. One of her pigtails had come undone. "Please?"

"No," I said again.

Harry and I waited outside in the cold night air for his mother. He made a snow angel in the yard, and I did, too. Then we lay still, side by side, waiting, gazing up at the sky.

And now I saw it. I saw the star. I saw it first.

"There it is." I pointed. "Mom's star!"

"What?" Harry asked.

"Mom's star," I repeated.

"What do you mean? How can it be your mom's star?"

The winter night was still. Trevor and Dad weren't there. There were no one else's memories of Mom, and no one else's words to tell about her.

I told the star story to Harry. I didn't use the same words that Trevor always did. They didn't seem right, now that it was *me* telling the story.

I chose my own words and I put them together in the way I wanted.

And when I got to the end of the story, it seemed right

to use the words my mother had said, the way Trevor always does:

*"Wherever I go, wherever I end up in this wide universe ...*

*Wherever you go, wherever you end up in this wide universe ...*

*That will be our star.*

*That's the one that will connect us."*

"Wow," Harry said softly. "That's so cool."

"Yeah," I agreed. It *was* cool. The star did connect us, and so did telling the story about the star. I couldn't remember that night, or Mom choosing the star, or her saying those words, but when I told the story about it, the story connected me to Mom and to Dad and Trevor. I wasn't left out, after all.

Harry and I lay there, two snow angels. We lay in the winter darkness, gazing up at Mom's star together.

# SPRING

# 1

## The Oyster

It was raining again. And cold.

I stared out the classroom window. It had been raining for days. I had pumped up the tires on my bicycle two weeks ago, when the last snow melted. But it was still too rainy and too cold to ride.

When would spring really come?

"Students!" Ms. Dean sounded excited. "Today, on this gloomy afternoon, we are going to learn something about a very special creature. A creature that always reminds me of winter turning to spring."

Ms. Dean put a poster on the board. We all laughed when we saw "the creature."

"A clam?" Harry asked.

"An oyster, actually. Not a clam," Ms. Dean grinned. "And you'll see why it reminds me of spring. Maybe it will end up reminding you of spring, too."

"Is it alive? It looks ... dead," said Jill, with a shudder.

"It does look dead," Ms Dean agreed, "but it isn't. An oyster has a hard shell on the outside."

She showed us another poster. "This shows the shell opened up. Like a snail, an oyster has a soft body on the inside." She pointed to it. "It also has an organ called a mantle, which uses minerals from the oyster's food to make a material called nacre. The oyster's shell is made from nacre."

We all stared at the squishy oyster body and the shiny shell.

"Sometimes a tiny something gets into the oyster's shell and irritates it," Ms. Dean told us. "It's like ... like getting a splinter in your finger, except the oyster can't get rid of it. It's there to stay."

I thought of Claire. She didn't seem to get sick as often on the days she was supposed to come to our house for dinner. Over the past three months, she'd gone into my room and colored on my star charts. She had hidden in the closet and jumped out at me, yelling "Boo!" She had followed me around the yard in her rain boots. Harry told me a few weeks ago that his family was going to have a new baby and he was excited. He wanted a little sister. I couldn't imagine anything worse. Another kid in the house? A younger one? It was bad enough having Claire around so much. Each time, after Claire went home, our house always seemed extra quiet, full of excellent empty spaces.

"So how does the oyster deal with this irritating, bothersome pest?" Ms Dean asked.

No one knew.

"The oyster creates more nacre. It covers the tiny irritating particle with layers of shiny shell. It keeps adding them until the particle is completely covered. These layers protect the oyster. The particle is still there, but it doesn't bother the oyster anymore."

That's pretty cool, I thought. I nudged Harry.

"Nice," he whispered.

"The layers don't just protect the oyster," said Ms. Dean, putting up a third poster. "Its layers also make something very special." She stepped back.

The picture showed an open oyster shell, with an oyster body inside, and—

"A pearl!" exclaimed Ms. Dean triumphantly.

The pearl was round, shiny, and white. It was beautiful.

Oysters *were* pretty amazing.

"And now do you see why oysters remind me of spring?" Ms. Dean asked. "In winter, everything looks dead, but out of the hard ground burst spring flowers. Oysters look dead ..."

I smiled. They look dead, but they aren't. And inside their rough, ugly shells, they have oozy oyster bodies that make shiny white pearls.

Harry grinned at me and I knew he got it, too. Suddenly, spring felt a little closer.

# 2

## An Announcement

*T*hat afternoon, soon after I got home from school, the rain finally stopped.

I ran outside and jumped onto my bike.

"I want you home at dinnertime," Dad yelled out the window to me. "I have something important to tell you and Trevor."

I rode through every delicious puddle. I skidded into every fresh mud slick. I made swervy tracks all the way up Harry's driveway.

Harry and I rode our bikes all the way to Cooper's Woods. On foot, we scouted for animal tracks. We hunted for snakes, and we turned over rocks, looking for slugs and millipedes. We climbed trees. We hiked to the edge of the fields and threw pebbles at the sagging scarecrow. When we saw Mr. Mutter feeding his pigs, we practiced spying on him. His dog, Barney, raised a lazy eyebrow at us. We raced back to our bikes and we rode some more.

Dad and Trevor were already sitting down to dinner when I came inside.

"Sorry," I said, but Dad didn't say anything about me being late. Trevor was talking about his wood-working project for school. Then I talked about oysters and pearls, and the snake, and the coyote tracks Harry and I had found in the woods. Dad didn't say much at all.

When we were done our meat loaf and potatoes, I got up to put my bike away, but Dad said, "Sit down, please, Patrick." He gave a little cough, cleared his throat. "I have an announcement."

"An announcement?" I repeated. The word sounded so formal.

Dad looked strange. He grinned; he bit his lip and frowned—and then he grinned again. "Yes, an announcement."

Suddenly, I felt nervous. I didn't sit down. I didn't want to.

Dad cleared his throat again. He said, "I asked Linda to marry me."

Linda. His friend.

"She said yes." Dad smiled like he was trying to keep it a medium smile, but it got away from him and spread across his whole face. "So she and Claire will be coming to live with us soon. At the end of August, before school starts, I hope."

Claire, the pest. Who always bugged me.

Dad's words stumbled along awkwardly. "I love Linda and I want her to be my wife. I hope we can all be happy here together."

"You're getting married?" I asked. "And they're going to come and live with us ... here?" I folded my arms.

Dad turned to me quickly. Nodded. "That's right." He kept nodding. "They'll come at the end of the summer, and we're planning the wedding for some time later." He started grinning again. An ear-to-ear grin. "Maybe December."

Claire, moving in here? It was impossible. There wasn't enough room. She would be into my things. She would be loud and she'd hang all over me.

"Where will Claire sleep?" I said. "There isn't room here for more people!"

"We'll make more room, Patrick," Dad said. "We'll renovate. I'm going to renovate. They'll be lots of room for all of us. We'll all fit fine."

But he was wrong. Trevor, Dad, and I already made a complete family. The house was fine already. Fine and full. Just enough people in just enough space.

Trevor frowned at me. Then he turned to Dad and smiled. "That's great news, Dad. I'm really happy for you. Congrats!"

"Thanks, Trevor," Dad said.

Trevor got up and went to Dad. He hugged him. Ever since Mom died, Trevor had tried to be perfect. Now he was doing it again. "Linda's really nice, Dad. And Claire seems cool, too."

Dad was grinning and hugging Trevor. "I'll turn our den into a little bedroom for Claire," he told me over Trevor's shoulder. "Don't worry. We'll make sure she's comfortable here. There's lots of room to share. You'll see."

I swallowed hard.

It wouldn't be fine, no matter what Dad said or did. I didn't want a stepmother, and I sure didn't want a little pesky stepsister.

"I need to put my bike away," I said. I left. And outside it was raining again.

# 3

## An Idea

As soon as I woke up the next morning, I remembered. I remembered that everything was going to change forever.

I got to school and Harry asked, "What's wrong?"

I shook my head. I didn't look at him.

"Nothing," I said.

That afternoon, when we did a reading circle, Sarah took my spot on the carpet.

"That's my place," I snapped at her. She looked up at me, surprised.

"I always sit there. You can't take my spot," I said.

Julie was sitting next to Sarah. "Patrick, it's not *your* spot," she said, making a face. "You don't own it."

I glared at them both. I turned and stomped away.

At lunchtime, we played soccer. Martin was shadowing me. He was too close. He was almost stepping on me. He was breathing down my neck.

I leaned into him. Pushed him suddenly, hard, and Martin fell.

"What's wrong with you?" Martin said angrily, rubbing his elbow.

"Nothing," I said.

The next day, Wednesday, it was the same.

I tried to forget about it. Forget that Linda and Claire were going to move in. But I couldn't.

It made everything bad. What good was spring, what good was summer, if Claire was coming in the fall?

Maybe I would run away. Maybe I would just leave. That would be a good idea.

Harry looked at me funny. "Are you okay?" he asked again on Thursday and Friday.

"Sure," I said.

The weekend came and went. I didn't want a stepmother, but more than anything, I didn't want a little sister. One brother, my dad, and me. And Mom. We were already a family. Two more people couldn't just squeeze their way in.

On Monday, another angry idea came. I'd get adopted by someone who lived all alone. Someone who wanted only one child. Who could be happy with just me. Maybe someone with a dog.

On Tuesday, another idea. If Linda and Claire were going to move into my house, crowd into my house, I'd move into *their* old house. I'd live there, and they could live here.

But why should I live all alone? It wasn't fair.

Then on Wednesday, a new idea. A better idea, piling on top of all the other ideas. Maybe I'd go and live with Harry. Harry would be surprised, all right, but he'd let me walk right in. He'd let me stay. I knew it. That was what best friends did.

All day, I thought about it, and the next day, too. I imagined it. It felt good, except for one thing. I'd be welcome in Harry's house, but what if I always felt like a visitor there, a guest? What if I never really felt at home? And, oh yeah, he'd be making room for a new baby soon.

So I thought and thought some more, and, on Friday, I got it. The big idea. The shiny, shimmery, best idea. The pearl.

A tree house. I would build a tree house.

I would build a tree house! It would be my own space and I'd use it whenever I wanted to get away from everything down here. That morning, I let Sarah sit in my spot on the carpet. When Martin crowded me during soccer, I didn't complain. In my tree house, I would stretch to the sky, spin around with my arms wide, and breathe in huge lungfuls of air. I'd live in the whole outdoors, all of it!

After school, I saw Harry. "Want to come over?" I asked.

"Sure," he shrugged.

Harry and I tromped through the field near my house. We blew grass between our fingers, trying to make it sing.

"So ... my dad and Linda are going to get married," I told him.

"Oh," he said, surprised.

"Not until winter. But they're moving in with us at the

end of the summer." It was the first time I'd said it out loud. It made it seem real. It made it hard to breathe.

"Oh," said Harry again.

He was looking at me. "Is Linda nice? She seems nice, the times I've met her."

I shrugged. Sometimes, when Linda read books to Claire, she gave each of the characters a special voice. Some were squeaky, some were grumbly, some were goofy. Linda liked to make Claire laugh.

Sometimes, when we were all listening to my dad tell one of his stories, I could tell Linda was looking at me, just her eyes resting on me, gently.

Sometimes, when Linda served slices of choco-late-chip banana cake, I ended up with the biggest one.

But mostly, I didn't know about her. I was trying to ignore her. "Nice? Yeah, maybe, but ..."

We blew on our grass some more. Harry made his sing. I couldn't.

"And Claire? She'll be coming, too, I guess," Harry said.

"Yeah," I said.

"Hey," Harry laughed. "Soon I'll have a baby brother

or sister in my family—and you'll have a new little sister, too! We'll both find out what it's like!"

I scowled. "I don't want to know what it's like. I already know it'll be too crowded," I complained. "I don't want them to come. There isn't room for us all."

"Right," Harry easily agreed. He made the grass sing again.

Then I remembered the pearl, my idea, all shiny and shimmery, and I grinned. I punched Harry in the arm.

"But, Harry, I have an idea. An excellent, excellent idea. I'm going to build a tree house!" I exclaimed.

"A tree house?" Harry's eyes lit up.

"Yeah," I said. "A tree house! It'll be great. I can live there. Or, if Dad says no, I can at least go there lots, when I need space. When I need to get away from Claire. It can be yours, too, if you want. And we can build it together; and we'll get Trevor to help."

"A tree house!" Harry repeated. A smile was spreading across his face.

"Will you help me?" I asked. "Will you help me build one this summer?"

"Will I?" Harry tossed away his grass blade and gave

my shoulder a shove. "Are you kidding?" He grabbed me and shook me until I had to shake him back, both of us grinning like goofs. "Of course, I will," he said. "What a great idea, Patrick. I will *definitely* help you build a tree house. Definitely!"

I laughed out loud. I knew I could count on Harry. Things were looking up.

# SUMMER

# 1

## The Tree

School was over and it was finally summer.

Usually summer was the best. Most summers, Harry and I swam in the pond and caught frogs along the creek. We hiked to the back of the fields and slid down the sandbank into the pit. We walked gingerly along the top fence rail, balancing with sticks, teetering. We lay in the hammock under the trees and read comics aloud to each other.

Most summers, Trevor and I drew a line in the dirt, challenging each other to knock down the pyramid of tin cans with one throw. Trevor showed me wrestling moves. Sometimes he hurt me by mistake, sometimes on purpose. Trevor taught me swear words as we weeded the vegetable garden. We told jokes as we fed the chickens and washed the truck.

When Dad came home from the hardware store at the end of each day, he made lemonade. We chewed on lemon slices while he barbecued outdoors in the breeze.

Most summers were lazy and hot. Most summers were the same, the days going on and on and never ending. Usually there was all the time in the world in the summer.

But this summer was already different. There was a big red circle around a number on the kitchen calendar. It was a day at the end of August. In just two months, Linda and Claire were moving in.

"I want to build the tree house as fast as we can," I told Harry. "So that by the time they come, I have somewhere else to go."

School was done, so Harry and I began our tree house project.

First, we had to find just the right tree. We wanted one that stood in the middle of many others. One that was tall—the tallest around, with many branches.

Harry and I walked through the forest, looking. We hiked along the paths made by the deer. We followed the riverbank and looked at the trees. Many were pine, green year round. They weren't right for a tree house. They had too many needles, too many branches spiraling around the trunk.

Small trees had branches that were too thin to support a tree house. Short trees weren't sturdy enough. Their branches weren't far enough off the ground for a tree house that soared into the sky.

Crowded trees had branches that clashed and criss-crossed. I looked at them and it made my chest feel tight. It made me think of our house with all of us in it: Dad and Trevor and Linda and Claire—and me. It made me think of the red-letter day on the calendar. It was less than two months away now.

We searched and searched. We spent every day in the forest. I could picture the perfect tree in my mind, but two weeks went by and Harry and I still hadn't found it. Maybe we never would.

We were on our bikes, riding beside Mr. Mutter's

fields. We didn't know where to look next.

Mr. Mutter waved his walking stick at us. "What are you lads up to?" he asked, friendly.

"Hello, Mr. Mutter," I said.

As Harry explained our project, I spun the pedals on my bike. I squeezed the brakes.

"Trees need sunlight. Their leaves use sunlight to make food," Mr. Mutter told us. He leaned against the rail fence. Barney yawned, flopped down between Harry and me, and raised a lazy eyebrow. "When trees grow close together in the forest, there isn't much space for their branches to grow out. There isn't much elbow room."

Mr. Mutter showed us, tucking his thumbs under his armpits and doing the chicken-wing flap. "But that doesn't mean they give up growing. It just means they have to grow in a different way. It just means that their branches have to reach up to find the sunlight."

He pointed between the trees. "If you want a tree that reaches out with its branches, try down there," he suggested. "Go straight that way."

It was Mr. Mutter's land in that direction. Usually, we

weren't supposed to go there.

"Thanks, Mr. Mutter," we told him.

He waved his walking stick. "Go on. Good luck!"

Barney sat up and wagged his tail at us.

Harry and I left our bikes. We climbed over the rail fence. We made our way through the trees, pushing at branches, stepping over logs and rocks.

We walked for quite a while.

I was excited, but there was still a knot in my stomach. What if we *never* found the perfect tree? A tree that was just the right height, with just the right branches, in just the right spot.

We kept moving, Harry in front.

I could picture the perfect family: Dad, Mom, Trevor, and me. Or now, at least, Dad, Trevor, and me. But just because you could picture the perfect thing, it didn't mean it was really out there, or that you could have it.

Ahead, the trees were thinning out. There was more sky between fewer branches. We stepped into a clearing. It was like a small, secret meadow. Wild grass grew tall. Two lilac trees grew near a pile of boulders. An old cabin or homestead must have stood there. There was even a little pond with a cluster of cattails. Trees rimmed the clearing. The sun beat down.

We stood and gazed. And then we saw it.

The tree wasn't where I thought it would be. It stood steady and alone on the edge of the forest. It wasn't as tall as I thought it would be. Others deeper in the forest were taller. It didn't have as many branches as I thought it would. It had three big, low branches and two higher ones. They extended out, into the sunshine, into the meadow. The tree had lots of space to grow.

We walked over to it. I touched its trunk, the bark furrowed and gnarled.

"This is it," said Harry.

"Yup," I agreed, and I grinned. Because perfect doesn't always end up matching the picture in your mind.

# 2

## Just Right

The next morning, Harry and I came back to the clearing. We climbed up into the tree as high as we could go. The world looked and sounded different. It even smelled different. There was room enough for everything up here.

Harry and I dangled our feet, leaning against the tree's trunk. We watched as the tree's shadow made the sunlight dance. We sat on every branch. We looked out at every view. We got to know our tree.

We climbed back down and walked around our tree. We tried to imagine what our tree house would look like, snug up there in the branches.

Then we got down to work, drawing up our plans. It

was fun but it took a long time. One day, three days, five days so far. It was the third week of July. As I hurried out of the house, I glanced at the calendar. August was on the very next page.

"Stick around," Dad suggested. He gestured with his mug of steaming coffee. "You can help me with some of those renovations."

But I shook my head. "Can't, Dad," I said as I jumped on my bike. "Have to work on the tree house."

"Patrick," he called, annoyed. I didn't look back. I didn't want to see the look of disappointment on Dad's face. I hurried away to meet Harry.

Two days later, Harry and I were finally ready to build. Trevor had a summer job, but he had agreed to help on weekends and some evenings. Sometimes having an older brother is good.

"We want to see in every direction," I told him. I spun in a circle, with my arms soaring outward. "So we'll build the tree house floor all the way around the trunk, and we'll put windows on every side."

"No problem," Trevor said, with a bow and a flourish. "Your wish is my command."

Harry and I laughed.

Dad had ordered lots of materials for his renovation. He had offered to get some for the tree house, too: planks of different lengths, nails, even extra tools. The three of us—Trevor, Harry, and I—worked hard all weekend. We carried all the materials into the forest. We even built the walls and roof of the tree house.

During the weekdays, Harry and I kept building. We left many empty spaces for doorways and windows. We made one large room. We made a balcony where Harry and I could sit together outside.

Trevor was at work in town all day long. He helped Dad a little with the renovations some evenings. But most nights, he ended up coming along to give us a hand. It was like he couldn't stay away.

"Go on. Go ahead," Dad told him. "Patrick needs help, too."

The three of us worked hard until the sun sank.

One week went by, then another, and another. Mostly, when we were working on our tree house, we were on top of the world. Sometimes, though, I made mistakes and Harry got angry. Or Harry made mistakes and

I got angry. On those days we both had lots of elbow room on the hike out to our bikes.

It was hard to divide the big room into two smaller rooms—one for me and one for Harry—but we did it.

Some days, even though we knew we didn't have time, Harry and I took long, lazy breaks. We couldn't resist. We wandered through the woods, exploring. We waded in the stream. We scouted out the trails that the deer made, and the coyotes.

One morning, around the middle of August, I asked Dad if he wanted to come and see the tree house.

"I wish I could," he told me. "But I'm behind on the renovations. And I need to make everything ready for when Linda and Claire arrive. I'm sorry, Patrick," he said. "Do you understand?" He looked worried.

"Sure," I said. And in a way, I did. Guess we both had a lot to do. Guess we were both watching that red circle on the calendar coming closer and closer. The difference was that he'd be happy when it got here, ready or not.

"Rain check?" he asked.

"Okay," I said.

And then, late one Wednesday evening, just before August ended, Dad's renovations were done.

"What do you think?" he asked me proudly. He flung open the door to our old den. "Do you think Claire will be happy here?"

I pretended to look in. A small desk. A bunk bed squeezed between the walls. That's where she would do homework. That's where she would sleep. The walls of the house seemed to press against me.

I shrugged. "Guess so, Dad," I said.

The very next day, just in time, the tree house was finished, too.

Harry and I climbed up and looked out across the tree tops.

From here, the world looked different. The world sounded different. The world even smelled different.

Up here, there was all the space in the world. Up here, there was room to breathe.

"What do you think?" Harry said proudly. "Great, isn't it?"

"Yeah," I replied. "It's great. It's just right."

# 3

## Claire

On Friday night, Claire came, and her mother. They moved in.

Dad put five potatoes in their skins on the barbecue. He did some chicken, too, and he boiled sweet carrots.

Dad and Linda, Trevor and Claire sat around the table on the porch. I sat on the front steps with the plate on my lap. I didn't talk much. I was thinking hard about my tree house, thinking about the plans, thinking about what more we needed to do.

I didn't look at Claire, and she had left me alone, for once. Elbow room.

The next morning, I was heading out to meet Harry, to go to the tree house for our first sleepover.

"Leaving so soon, Patrick? Hey, why don't we all come with you? Give you a hand with your things. Help you set up for the night," Dad suggested. "I know Claire would like to see your tree house, and I certainly would, too." He shook his head. "I can't believe I haven't even seen it yet!"

Dad looked at me, hopeful, and maybe a little guilty. Linda was looking at me, too. Not hopeful but *more* than that. Like she was sure that I would make things right.

Claire was sitting at the kitchen table, coloring. Her hair fell forward, covering her face.

"Claire?" Linda asked gently. "Do you want to go and see Patrick's tree house?"

I was halfway out the door, almost away from here. Dad hadn't wanted to come before now, and it was okay for him to see it, finally. But I didn't want Claire to come. I just didn't.

Claire lifted her face, looked at me, and I looked back.

"No," she said quickly. She looked back down at her paper. "No, I think I want to finish this."

I knew she didn't mean it. I knew she wanted to see the tree house. And I thought about telling her she could come along. Maybe I was that kind of guy.

But I just couldn't let go of this tight feeling inside. I knew it wasn't Claire's idea to live with us. I knew it wasn't her fault. But here she was, crowding her way in, her and her mom. Now there'd always be less room. Less time with Dad and Trevor. Less space for memories of Mom.

I turned.

Dad followed me outside. "So, you be careful there, Patrick," he said. He watched me strap my sleeping bag onto my bike. "Have you got your walkie-talkie? I want to hear from you boys this afternoon, and then this evening, and then first thing in the morning." He looked worried.

I nodded, not meeting his eyes. "Okay, Dad."

He didn't say anything for a minute. I hoisted up my backpack.

"You know, Patrick, I love you. I'll miss you today and tonight," he said.

"Okay," I said, surprised.

"Patrick, I haven't talked to you much about my marriage to Linda, about them moving in with us. I guess I was afraid of what you might say. I thought if I waited, you'd just come around. Get to know Linda. Get to like Claire," Dad said. "Like Trevor has."

I got on my bike.

"I'm sorry. For not talking to you about all this a long time ago."

"Okay, Dad," I said quickly. I put my foot on the pedal, gave a push. "I'm going to head out now."

He waved as I rode away.

I met Harry at the end of his road. We rode our bikes to Mr. Mutter's land, and then began the hike into the clearing. All our visits had made a path, like we belonged here.

"Did they come?" Harry asked over his shoulder. "Linda and Claire?"

"Yeah," I said. I banged my stick on the tree trunks as we passed, banged it hard.

Harry didn't talk about them anymore after that.

The rest of the day was good, really good.

Being in the tree house was like being in another world. Harry and I yelled at the top of our lungs. We spotted shapes in the clouds and we squinted into the distance, imagining we saw smoke signals. We ran in the field, arms flung wide, and we watched birds, silent and still. We threw stones at targets. We did somersaults and collapsing cartwheels. We inhaled lunch and we wolfed down dinner. I walkie-talkied Dad once, and then again as evening came.

Harry and I carried soft pine branches up into the tree house. We spread out our sleeping bags on them.

We went to sleep with the smell of pine surrounding us, and the stars shining down.

The summer was almost over.

Next day, Sunday, we rode our bikes home, and then the following day was Monday, the very last day of the summer holidays.

One last summer day at the tree house.

Dad came into my room early, before I was even out of bed.

"Patrick, I know you're trying to get used to all the changes around here. I know it's hard for you, but Claire is only seven and it's difficult for her, too. She said no before, but I want you to show her the tree house," he told me. "It might cheer her up. It might help her feel more at home. She said no before. But this time, she has to go, today. You have to take her, and I think it's best if you do it alone, you and Harry, without me along."

I wanted my dad to come, not Claire. I didn't want Claire anywhere near the tree house. It made me feel like crying. But my dad didn't wait for me to say it was all right. After I ate breakfast, Dad helped Claire get her bike out of our shed. He watched while we rode away.

I rode my bike ahead fast, dust kicking up behind. Claire trailed after me, following.

Harry was waiting on the fence by his laneway, as usual. He waved as we got close.

"Hi Patrick. Hi Claire."

He made his bike rear like a horse, neighed, and Claire smiled a little.

"Let's go," I grumbled, riding ahead.

We rode down the path to Mr. Mutter's land until we got to the right place along the rail fence.

"Put your bike here," Harry told Claire, showing her.

Soon after, Harry and I and Claire were heading down

the path. For once, I was in front. I walked on, didn't look back.

Harry called, "Wait. Wait for Claire."

I picked up a handful of pebbles. I threw them at a squirrel. One, two, three.

Down the path, through the trees. "This way," Harry was saying to Claire, just like she was his little sister.

I picked up a stick. I hit the bushes with it as I walked. *Wap! Wap! Wap!*

And when we came to the clearing, there it was. The tree house.

The sun shone down. The leaves on the tree were still green. The branches were wide and welcoming. The tree house was there, open to the sky.

Looking at it, I could breathe.

I walked toward it and put my hand on the bark. And behind me, I heard Claire speak.

"Your tree house hugs the tree," she said softly.

And I guess she was right.

So ... she saw the tree house, and I'd done what Dad had asked me to do.

Now Harry said to me softly, at my shoulder, "Aren't

we going up? Aren't we going to take her up?"

"No," I said.

And so we turned around again and walked back out the path to our bikes.

"Who's that?" Claire asked Harry, pointing.

There was Mr. Mutter leaning on the rail fence, swinging his walking stick. We hadn't seen him all summer.

"Hello, boys," he greeted us. "Hello! How did your tree hunt go?"

"Good," Harry replied enthusiastically. "We found just the right tree, in the clearing. Just where you said." Mr. Mutter nodded, pleased. "And we built our tree house. It's fantastic. You should go and have a look sometime."

"Good, good," Mr. Mutter said, nodding.

But now Barney was sniffing Claire's hand, and Mr. Mutter was asking me, "Who's your new friend? Who's this charming little girl?"

I shrugged. I got on my bike.

Harry nudged her encouragingly. "I'm Claire," she said.

I turned my back on them all, said, "Goodbye, Mr. Mutter," and pedaled away.

# AUTUMN

# 1

## Drawing

School started on the next day, Tuesday. Linda took Claire that first day and waited for her after school, too. She did it on the second day, Wednesday, as well.

But on Thursday and Friday, because of her work, Linda couldn't take Claire to school or bring her home.

So I took Claire with me on the bus to school, like Dad asked. And I waited for her after school, like Dad asked.

"You're a good boy," Dad told me, ruffling my hair. "Thanks, Patrick."

Claire trailed silently behind me. Down the driveway to where we got on the bus, and back up the driveway again.

"Here," I said. I showed her where the cookies were. The milk. The crackers and cheese.

But she just said, "No, thanks," and went right upstairs. To her room, I guess.

I didn't know, because that first week, as soon as I could, I went to the tree house. I climbed up the ladder. I looked out into the distance as far as I could see. I took deep breaths. I spread my arms and stretched.

I did my homework there. I sat on the platform and dangled my feet over the edge. I lay back and looked at the leaves on our tree.

On Saturday, Harry came to the tree house, too. We were there all the day long. We made plans. We talked about getting a rope and hanging it from a branch, making a swing. We drew pictures of how it could look. Then we looked in the woods for a big tree stump that we could turn into a table. We looked for smaller stumps that we could turn into stools.

On Sunday, it rained. Trevor asked Claire if she wanted to play Snakes and Ladders, but she said no. Linda asked Claire if she wanted to go grocery shopping with her and Dad, but she said no. When Linda and Dad came back, Dad asked Claire if she wanted to help make the apple crisp for dessert, but she said no.

She just sat at the kitchen table all day long, and it looked like she was drawing.

All the next week, as well, I walked Claire back and forth from the school bus. And all those mornings, and after-school afternoons, and all those evenings, she still didn't run around the house and make a lot of noise. She didn't mess up my stuff. She didn't kick me under the table while we ate.

It was weird. Now that she was living here, she seemed different. Not as much of a pest.

I don't know what she was doing instead of all those annoying things. But when Harry came over after school on Friday, she was sitting at the kitchen table again, drawing.

Harry stood, looking over her shoulder.

"Hey, Claire," Harry said. "That's really good!"

She didn't say anything.

"I mean it, Claire," he said. He nudged her. "You're an *artiste*," he said with a grin, "which is *artist* in French," and he nudged her again. "Your drawing is really good!"

Claire giggled, squirming away from his elbowing. "Stop it!" she complained, grinning. "You're tickling me!"

"Come and look, Patrick," Harry called to me. "It's really cool." But I muttered, "That's okay," and continued up the stairs.

Later that night, I did see it, though. It came under my door, a flat piece of paper, no folds, covered in pencil markings and eraser shavings. Claire had titled it *Patrick's Tree House*. She had drawn the tree house so it looked like it was hugging the tree. No, more than that. It looked like it was growing right out of the tree, like it was part of the tree itself.

I didn't like Claire or her mom living here. I felt like I'd lost my home. But at least I had the tree house.

I looked at the drawing for a long time. Harry was right. It was really cool. It made me smile. I felt good just looking at it.

Good but bad, too.

Bad because Claire had made it for me, and I guess she'd lost her home, too. And even though I had the tree house and she had nothing, Claire was trying to make me feel better. And I was just trying to make her feel worse.

## 2

### Going Home

On Saturday, Harry and I spent the day at the tree house again. "Come for dinner," I said to Harry as we rode toward home.

That night was quiet and still. After dinner, Trevor went upstairs to watch television. Dad was reading. Harry and I played chess. One game, two. It was getting late, but we started our third game.

Harry yawned. His arms were crossed over the table and his chin rested on his fists. He yawned so hard, his eyes closed.

I yawned back. My elbow was on the table, my head propped up on my fist. I was tired, too. I was so tired, I couldn't remember if I was waiting for him to move or he was waiting for me.

"Your turn, slowpoke," he said.

"Okay." I moved my queen. Then I shut my eyes for a moment, just to rest them.

It was so quiet. It was like being alone, just Dad, Trevor, me—and Harry, of course. It was just like it used to be.

I rubbed my eyes. Maybe we would take a star walk tonight.

In the dreamy silence, I heard Linda say, "Time to go home, I think."

I'd almost forgotten they were here. I *had* forgotten they were here.

Linda was saying it was time to go home, I realized sleepily, and, of course, it was time for them to go home, back home, to their own home. Yes, that's where everyone wanted to be on a drowsy, cozy night like this one. Home. In your home. Just you and your very own family.

Claire thought so, too. Because I saw her look up from her book, look up quickly, right into her mother's face.

"Home?" she asked, her sleepy voice lifting.

She was going home! I could see the idea sparkling in her eyes.

"Yes, it's time for Harry to go home, honey." Linda put her hand gently on Claire's shoulder and stroked her hair.

It was time for Harry to go home, of course, not Claire.

"Look at the boy," Linda said to Dad. "He's almost falling asleep playing chess with Patrick."

"You're right, dear," my dad was agreeing. "I'll drive you home, Harry," he said, and he gathered up my sleepy friend. Linda was going upstairs with Claire to get her ready for bed, and then I was going upstairs, too.

But when I climbed into my bed and I closed my eyes, I couldn't fall asleep. I couldn't stop seeing the look on Claire's face. She wanted to be home, in her own home. She wanted to be where she belonged.

I closed my eyes but I couldn't fall asleep. Not for a really long time.

# 3

## Room for All

*I*n the morning, I jumped on my bike. Dad came out onto the porch with his coffee. The leaves on the trees were starting to change color. Some had fallen in the night. Red, yellow, orange on edges of the farm fields.

"Harry and I are going to the tree house," I told him.

"Okay, buddy," he said. "And, hey—thanks for helping out with Claire, taking her back and forth from school. It's helped us all to get settled. Linda and I have both made some changes to our schedules so we can help out more with that."

I nodded. "Sure. See you later, Dad."

The air was crisp. It said summer was ending and autumn was here.

Harry was waiting for me on the top rail of the fence. He saw me coming from a long way off and he waved, a big wide arc with his arm.

I pedaled up and braked hard, making a beautiful sliding skid.

"Nice," Harry said admiringly.

I grinned. "Harry, I have another idea," I told him. "There's something we have to do."

"Sure," said Harry.

I hesitated. "We have to build another room in the tree house," I told him. I looked down. I paused, trying to think of how I would explain.

"For Claire," he said. Almost, but not quite, a question.

I nodded. Grinned. "Right. For Claire." He understood. Of course he did. He was my best friend.

So we began that day, that Sunday.

And on Monday, I told Claire we needed her help with the tree house after school. That we were building a new room for it. She could carry some of the tools and materials, and hand Harry and me the things we needed. The new room was for her, after all, so the least she could do was help out.

The autumn leaves shimmered. The air was all sunlight and shadows dancing.

The days went by: Monday, Tuesday, Wednesday, Thursday. We went to school and we worked on the tree house. Then, on Friday, we were done.

"Come on up," I said to Claire.

"Okay," she agreed. Eyes sparkling, she climbed the ladder.

The three of us, Harry, Claire, and I, stood in the tree house. Our pearl. We looked out across the tree tops. From here, we could see that the sky went on forever.

I smiled. Here, Claire and I could stretch out wide, and Harry, too. There was plenty of room for all of us.

Photo credit: Georgia Coles

# Interview with Susan Hughes

**Can you tell me how this story began for you?**

I wanted to write a story about a tree house. I saw this image: a boy in a tree house amongst the green of the leaves and the blue of the sky. The idea came to me that the tree house would be a special refuge for the boy. A place he needs to build because he is feeling "crowded" at home, uncertain that there is enough room for him in his father's affections, uncertain that there is space at home for memories of his mother. The tree house would hug the trunk of the tree but open out into endless space. A place with room for him and for his best friend. A place that, ultimately, the boy decides he must share with a new person in his life.

**As you began to write this story, did you picture it happening in a place you know—and, if so, where is that place?**

Yes, I did. My mother grew up in Colpoy's Bay, a farming community on the Bruce Peninsula near Wiarton, and her parents continued to live there throughout their lives. My siblings and I loved it when my parents would take us to visit. Each season was special. In the spring, we'd wander down to the creek, amazed at the torrential rush of water into the bay below. We'd roam the pastures in the summer, trying to ignore the stares of the curious cows—and avoid stepping in their pats!—as we explored the "castle," the ruins of the neighbor's barn and silo. In the fall, we'd stuff our pockets with chestnuts picked up along the roadside and, on our way back from the corner store, pop black gumballs into our mouths, one after another after another. In the winter, we'd dig forts into the towering snow banks and go sledding down the sides of the sand pit in the back field.

**Did you ever build a tree house there?**

No, we had lots of other types of fun, but we never built a tree house. The farmhouse was surrounded by fields. There was one large sheltering tree behind the house, not suitable for a tree house, but it did have a swing—a wooden slat hung from two thick scratchy ropes—which we took turns on, pushing one another under the shade of the branches. Sometimes the pusher would help twirl the swing—twirling it round and round until the ropes were so tightly wound that the seat was lifted up and the swinger's feet dangled high above the ground—and then a big *push!* The swing would whip around and around, in crazy spinning dizzying circles while we screamed. How we loved that!

**In the end, Patrick stops just thinking of himself and comes to realize how Claire feels. What do you think brings about this change of heart in Patrick?**

Once Patrick's tree house is built, he still worries about the changes happening in his house and in his family, about being crowded out of his father's life, about his family memories of his mother being lost. He still feels hurt. He still feels that he has lost his home.

But over time, as Patrick stands in his tree house and stretches and breathes, he begins to feel better, less afraid. He is able to look beyond himself. He has been upset with Claire, and mean to her, shutting her out. But now he is able to see that they share something important. Claire has also lost her home. However, although she has lost as much, or more, than him, she is trying to make Patrick feel better. And when he receives her special drawing of his tree house, he realizes that she doesn't have anything like a tree house to help her cope with the changes in her life.

Yes, having the new tree house has changed Patrick. He now feels like he needs to reach out to Claire, to show her that there is room for her in his special place.

**Why does Patrick call the tree house "our pearl" on the very last page of the story?**
Well, I'm going to answer your question by asking you some questions!

Think back to the chapter titled "Oyster" in the Spring section. Do you remember that Patrick's teacher, Ms. Dean, explains that an oyster forms layers to protect itself from any irritating particles? She also says that the layers make something very special, a pearl.

Later, in the chapter titled "An Idea," Patrick is upset that Claire, irritating Claire, is going to be moving into his house. He is trying to decide what to do. He has many ideas which come one after the other, piling up one on top of the other, layer after layer. His big idea, his "shiny, shimmery, best idea," is to build a tree house. Did you notice that he calls this idea "the pearl"?

Does this help you answer the question about why he later also calls the tree house "our pearl"?

**What suggestions do you have for young writers as they work on their stories?**

My advice to other writers is always the same: Read, read, read. Write, write, write. Just do it. When you're beginning a story, don't worry too much about how good the story is or how perfect the words are. Get it down on the page. Don't even worry about starting at the beginning. Jumping in anywhere is okay. You can add the beginning and the end when you like.

When you're done, take a break from the story. Set it aside. Let it cool down. Come back to it again later and read it with fresh eyes. You'll probably want to make changes, tweaks, revisions. Go for it. And repeat again.

At some point, you'll read it and you'll be overcome with that most amazing feeling of: "Hey! I like it. I don't want to change one word of it."

Guess what? Your story is done!

**Thank you, Susan**